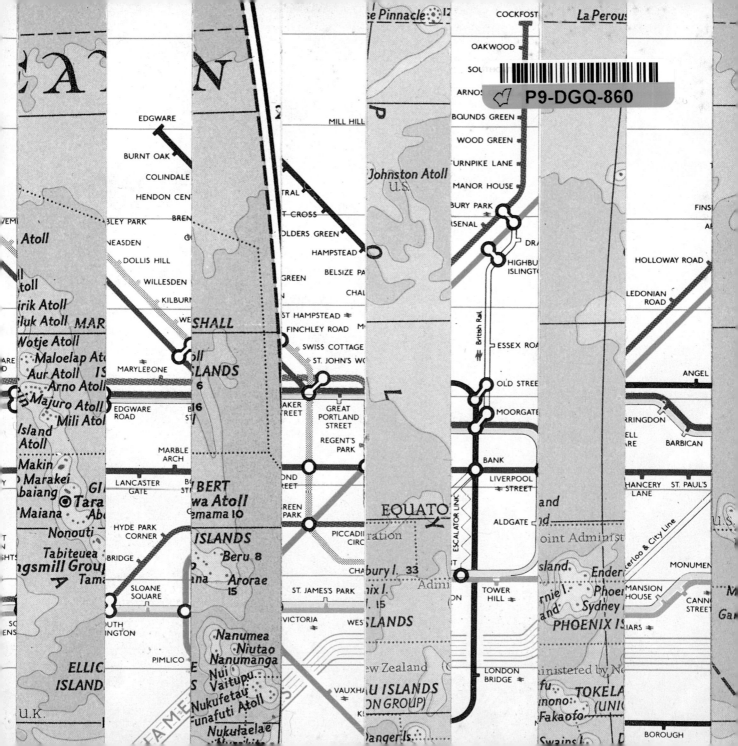

GRIFFIN & SABINE

Turning and turning in...

GRIFFIN&SABINE

An Extraordinary Correspondence

Written and Illustrated
by
Nick Bantock

Chronicle Books · San Francisco

Bantock, Nick.
Griffin & Sabine : an extraordinary correspondence / written and
illustrated by Nick Bantock.
    p.   cm.
ISBN 0-87701-788-3
  I. Title.   II. Title: Griffin and Sabine.
PR6052.A54G75 1991
823'.914–dc20   90-26484
                      CIP

Distributed in Canada by
Raincoast Books, 112 East Third Avenue,
Vancouver, B.C., V5T 1C8

10 9

Chronicle Books
275 Fifth Street
San Francisco, California 94103

For Kim Kasasian

Griffin Moss
It's good to get in touch
with you at last.
Could I have one of your
fish postcards?
I think you were right—
the wine glass has more impact
than the cup.
                Sabine Strohem

P.O. Box 1. Katie. Sicmon Islands. South Pacific.

Griffin Moss. Gryphon Cards
41 Yeats Avenue
London
N.W. 3
England.

22 FEB

SABINE
THANK YOU FOR YOUR EXOTIC
POSTCARD. FORGIVE ME IF
IT'S A MEMORY LAPSE ON MY
PART, BUT SHOULD I KNOW
YOU?
I CAN'T FATHOM OUT HOW YOU
WERE AWARE OF MY FIRST,
BROKEN CUP, SKETCH FOR THIS
CARD. I DON'T REMEMBER
SHOWING IT TO ANYONE.
PLEASE ENLIGHTEN ME.

YOURS
GRIFFIN MOSS

Drinking Like a Fish

GRYPHON CARDS

SABINE STROHEM
P.O. BOX ONE F
KATIE
SICMON ISLANDS
SOUTH PACIFIC

By air mail
Par avion

Griffin Moss

No, Griffin, you don't know me, not
in the way you mean, though I've
been watching your art for many years.
Having finally established who and
where you are, I feel compelled to
reveal myself.

The phenomenon that links us has taught me much
about you, yet I am ignorant of your history.
Please tell me something of your life.

It is such a pleasure having your images in a
tangible form. I really like the kangaroo in the hat,
but I wonder whether you should have darkened
the sky ?
                                              Sabine

Griffin Moss
41 Yeats Avenue
London
N.W. 3
England

Kangaroo with a Red Hat

MS. STROHEM   15 MARCH
WHAT'S GOING ON? HOW IN THE WORLD
COULD YOU KNOW I DARKENED THE SKY
BEHIND THE KANGEROO? IT WAS ONLY A
LIGHT COBALT FOR ABOUT HALF AN HOUR.
AND WHAT DO YOU MEAN BY "PHENOMENON"
AND TANGIBLE"?
OK. IF GETTING ME INTRIGUED IS WHAT
YOU'RE AFTER, YOU'VE SUCCEEDED, BUT
YOU CAN HARDLY EXPECT ME TO SPILL MY
LIFE STORY TO A STRANGER.
WHY ARE YOU BEING SO RUDDY
MYSTERIOUS?

        GRIFFIN MOSS

        GRYPHON CARDS

P.S. YOUR POSTCARDS ARE
HANDMADE - DID YOU DO THEM
YOURSELF?

Air Mail   Par avion

SABINE STROHEM
PO BOX ONE F
KATIE
SICMON 1545.
SOUTH PACIFIC

Griffin – you're right. I am being mysterious, but I assure you it's for good reason. What I have to say will be disturbing, and I wish you no distress.

I share your sight. When you draw and paint, I see what you're doing while you do it. I know your work almost as well as I know my own. Of course I do not expect you to believe this without proof :

Last week while working on a head in chalk, you paused and lightly sketched a bird in the bottom corner of the paper. You then erased it, and obliterated all trace with heavy black. Don't be alarmed – I wish you only well.

Yes the pictures on the cards are mine.

Sabine

Griffin Moss
41 Yeats Avenue
London
N.W. 3
England.

SABINE   16 APRIL

THIS IS IMPOSSIBLE, AND YET IT MUST BE TRUE.
THERE WAS NO ONE IN MY STUDIO ALL THAT WEEK,
LET ALONE WHEN I SCRIBBLED THE BIRD. I'VE
CHECKED THE DRAWING AND THERE'S NOT THE
SLIGHTEST SIGN OF THE CREATURE FRONT OR
BACK. GOD KNOWS HOW, BUT YOU REALLY CAN
SEE ME, CAN'T YOU?
WHY DOESN'T THIS ALARM ME AS MUCH AS IT
SHOULD? I SUPPOSE BECAUSE I'VE ALWAYS
SENSED THAT I WAS BEING WATCHED, BUT I'D PUT IT
DOWN TO EVERYDAY PARANOIA.
I'VE A MILLION QUESTIONS. AM I
THE ONLY ONE YOU SEE? WHAT FORM
DOES YOUR SIGHT TAKE?
HOW COME I CAN'T SEE YOU?

GRYPHON CARDS

I WANT TO HEAR EVERYTHING.
WRITE IN DETAIL. TELL ME ALL
ABOUT YOURSELF. I DEMAND
TO KNOW — PLEASE.

GRIFFIN

SABINE STROHEM
P.O. BOX IF
KATIE
SICMON ISLANDS
SOUTH PACIFIC

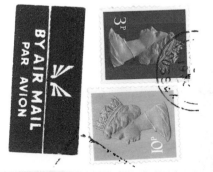

BY AIR MAIL
PAR AVION

3P

10P

AIR 7 7

QUEPOL

Griffin Moss
41 Yeats Avenue
London
N W 3
England

You probably won't have
heard of our islands —
they're no more than specks
of dust in standard
atlases....

the Siccmon Islands

Arbah
Katie
Katin
Hafmon
Sea
Ta Fin
Quepol
Typ

Pacific

Arbah: The fishing port
were May, my childhood
sweetheart grew up.
Katie: Home
                    islands
Katin: Seat of th
            work place.
concil and me
            < forest. I've
Ta Fin: Th
            there 3 times.
been los
        ol: Island of water.
Qur
    p: Houses the great
arved wooden lighthouse.

From: Griffin Moss
41 Yeats Avenue
London NW3

SPECIAL DELIVERY
SD-8
23-10-61
EXPRÈS

Griffin – Can you imagine what it would be like never to see the back of your hand. Then quite suddenly to turn it over and gaze at it? I read your letter again and again, nodding to myself as the events in your life matched my memory of the way you were painting. When I read of Vereker's death and your misery, I found it hard to breathe. And hearing that my existence eased your pain made my heart race. We have found one another, and I give thanks. Take care Griffin.
I will, I promise, tell you more of the islands and my work when next I write.

Sabine

Griffin Moss
41 Yeats Avenue
London NW3
England

JULY 3

SABINE

TODAY I PHONED THE
PLACE IN DUBLIN WHERE
THEY KEEP THE RECORDS
OF BIRTHS AND DEATHS. MY
TWIN THEORY IS BLOWN — I WAS
DEFINITELY A SINGLE BIRTH. I
ALSO DID A BIT OF RESEARCH ON
TELEPATHY — THERE WAS A MAN
AND HIS DAUGHTER IN ARGENTINA
BEFORE THE FIRST WAR WHO
SUPPOSEDLY COULD DO IDENTICAL
DRAWINGS WHILST MILES APART.
IT SOUNDS DUBIOUS TO ME AND
ANYWAY, I PREFER TO THINK OF
US AS UNIQUE.

YOUR PICTURES - THE ONES ON THE CARDS — SEEM VERY SLIGHTLY
FAMILIAR. MAYBE I CAN SEE YOUR WORK TOO, ONLY MY RECEPTION
(AS IT WERE) ISN'T AS GOOD AS YOURS?
WINTER'S HERE EARLY. THE CITY IS GREY AND DREARY. I CHEER MYSELF
BY DAYDREAMING OF YOU AND THE SOUTH SEAS.

LOVE GRIFFIN

GRYPHON CARDS

EXPRESS

VIA AIR MAIL
CORREO AEREO
PAR AVION

8ᴾ   1½ᴾ

SABINE STROHEM
PO BOX 1 F
KATIE
SICMON ISLANDS
SOUTH PACIFIC

Man Descending a Staircase

AIR

AIR   AIR

KATIN   7

Griffin Moss
41 Yeats Avenue
London NW3
England.

AIR   AIR

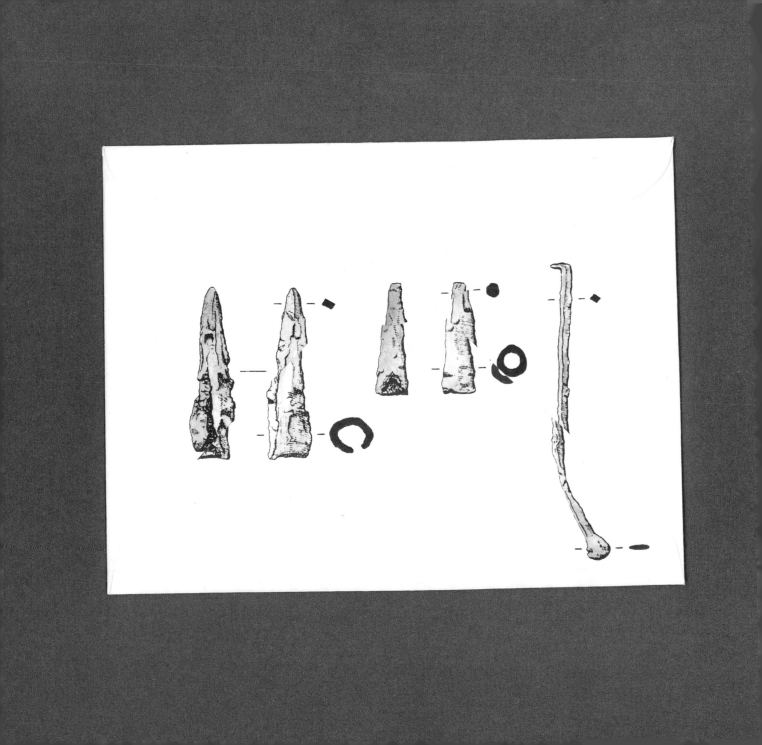

SABINE STROHEM

PO BOX ONE F

KATIE

SICMON ISLANDS

SOUTH PACIFIC

VIA AIR MAIL

From: Griffin Moss
41 Yeats Avenue
London
NW3

EXPRESS

Griffin– I had failed to understand how unhappy you are. You cover up with jokes and a front of being self-contained. I'm worried for you. Don't judge yourself so harshly. Why not get down from the white horse, take off the armour, and walk away from the uninterested maidens?

So — you've been making love to me ten thousand miles away—how tantalizing. *

It accounts for the extreme potency of those drawings. I'll have to find a way to return the affection

Remember to be gentle with yourself —

Griffin Moss
41 Yeats Avenue
London NW3
England
.

— Sabine

SABINE   SEPT 29
WHEN YOU FOUND ME, I
THOUGHT MY LONELINESS
HAD GONE FOR GOOD. I WAS
KIDDING MYSELF.
I DESPERATELY DESIRE YOUR
COMPANY. I HAVEN'T TALKED TO
ANYONE IN THREE DAYS.
I WAS SURE I WAS GOING TO START
SEEING YOUR PICTURES LIKE YOU
SEE MINE. I'VE TRIED SO HARD. I'VE
CONCENTRATED, I'VE MEDITATED,
I'VE DONE EVERYTHING EXCEPT
STAND ON MY HEAD, & I GET NOTHING.
NOT A FLICKER. AND I THINK MY
OWN WORK IS GOING STALE.
I HAVEN'T PRODUCED ANYTHING
WORTHWHILE FOR WEEKS —
AND MY STOMACH HURTS. PATHETIC ISN'T IT (AREN'T I)?
SEND ME SOMETHING FROM THE ISLANDS. SOMETHING MAGIC THAT
WILL HEAL MY AILING SOUL.
HOW CAN I MISS YOU THIS BADLY WHEN WE'VE NEVER MET?
                                    LOVE GRIFFIN

Frankie and Johnny

GRYPHON CARDS

SABINE STROHEM
P.O. BOX ONE F
KATIE
SICMON ISLS.
SOUTH PACIFIC

Air Mail Par avion

13ᵖ

Griffin – I miss you too.

If you don't see my pictures there's a good reason. Sometimes willpower alone cannot make things happen.

As for your work being stale, I disagree. What I see is not staleness, it's change. I feel you moving to your dark side. Give your shadow a chance to unveil itself. You said that Gryphon cards was dedicated to your perception of the universe — then let the cards reflect the night.

Island magic works on Island souls. You and I will heal each other.

Sabine

Griffin Moss, 41 Yeats Av.
London NW3 England.

NOV 24

SABINE,
THIS PLACE IS WEARING
ME DOWN. I FIND IT HARDER
AND HARDER TO GET UP IN
THE MORNING, I NEVER USED
TO BE LIKE THIS. I WAS ALWAYS
DISGUSTINGLY BRIGHT AS SOON AS
MY EYES OPENED. I'VE STARTED
TO HATE THIS CITY, THIS COUNTRY
ALL THESE STUPID FUCKING PEOPLE.
I ALMOST GOT INTO A FIGHT IN A
CAFE YESTERDAY. I WAS SICK OF
BEING ALTERNATELY IGNORED &
ABUSED BY THE WAITER AND
WAITRESS. I WAS OVERTAKEN BY
AN ANGER LIKE NOTHING I'VE EVER
EXPERIENCED BEFORE. I STARTED YELLING AND KICKING CHAIRS. I GUESS
I FINALLY SNAPPED.
MY DAYS ARE BARREN BUT MY NIGHTS ARE HEADY WITH YOU.
I WANT TO KNOW WHAT YOU LOOK LIKE. WILL YOU SEND ME A
PHOTOGRAPH?

The Blind Leading the Blind

GRYPHON CARDS

SABINE STROHEM
PO BOX IF. / KATIE
SICMON ISLANDS
SOUTH PACIFIC

AIR PAR AVION MAIL

ALL MY LOVE GRIFFIN

Griffin – A photograph would not be possible. I offer myself in paint instead. It's self-flattering, but that's our prerogative as artists – to record ourselves the way we wish. Why, my kindred spirit, are you prepared to settle for a postcard of my face? If you wish to see me, why not come here? What is there to stop you – you're clearly unhappy where you are.
Come.

Sabine

Griffin Moss
41 Yeats Avenue
London NW3
England

JAN 1

GRYPHON CARDS

SABINE
THINGS HAVE BECOME SO
DIFFICULT. I MUSTN'T WRITE
AGAIN. THIS WHOLE AFFAIR HAS
GOTTEN TOO INTENSE. TOO REAL
SABINE, YOU DON'T EXIST.
I INVENTED YOU. YOU, THE CARDS,
THE STAMPS, THE ISLANDS, YOU'RE
A FIGMENT OF MY IMAGINATION.
I WAS LONELY AND I WANTED A
FRIEND. BUT I'M ALMOST OUT OF
CONTROL. I'VE STARTED TO THINK
I'M IN LOVE WITH YOU.
BEFORE IT TAKES ME OVER IT HAS
TO STOP.
GOODBYE.

GRIFFIN

Pierrot's Last Stand

Griffin

Foolish man. You cannot turn me
into a phantom because you are
frightened. You do not dismiss a muse
at whim. 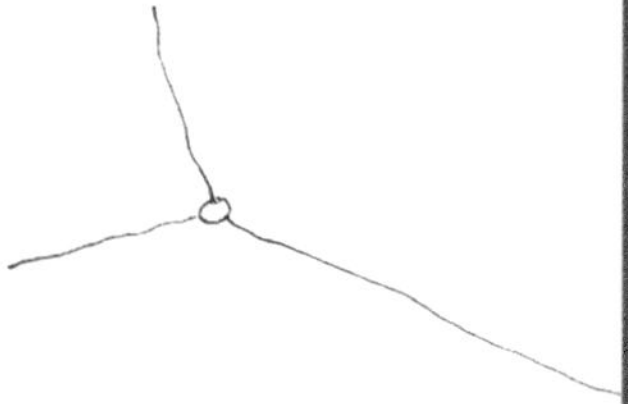
If you will not join me —
then I shall come to you.

Sabine

. . The ceremony of innocence . . .

These postcards and letters were found pinned to the ceiling of the otherwise empty studio of Griffin Moss.

Griffin Moss is missing.

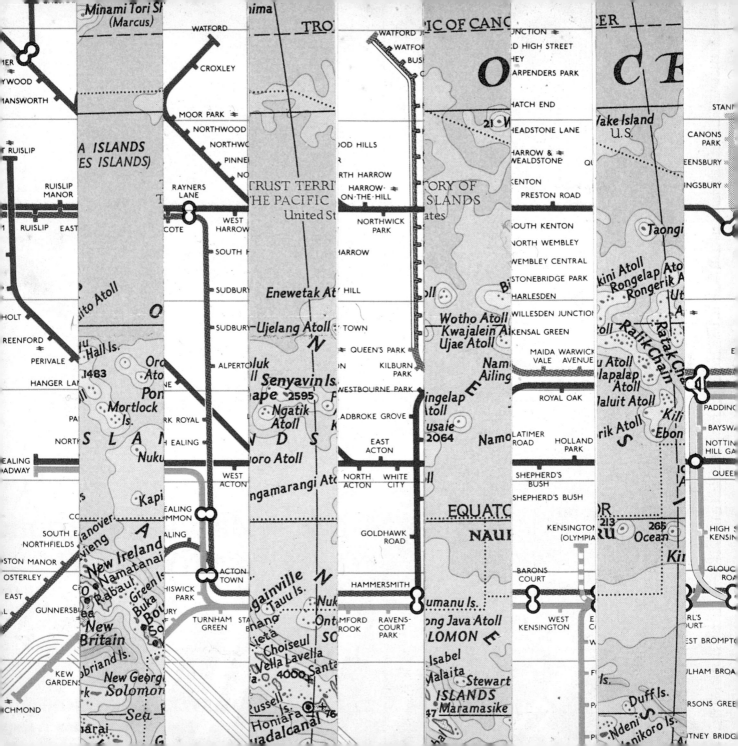